The Lucky Star

Written by Judy Young and Illustrated by Chris Ellison

SLEEPING BEAR PRESS
TALES *of* YOUNG AMERICANS SERIES

For Ross,
who is my lucky and guiding star.

Judy

★

To my family, who have always been my lucky stars.

Chris

Sleeping Bear Press®
310 North Main Street, Suite 300
Chelsea, MI 48118
www.sleepingbearpress.com

Printed and bound in China.

First Edition

10 9 8 7 6 5 4 3 2 1

Library of Congress Cataloging-in-Publication Data

Young, Judy.
The lucky star / written by Judy Young ; illustrated by Chris Ellison.
p. cm.
Summary: In 1933, facing the hardships of the Great Depression, Ruth learns to follow her mother's example and count her lucky stars when she turns her disappointment over not being able to attend fifth grade into a blessing for her younger sister.

ISBN 978-1-58536-348-3

1. Depressions—1929—Juvenile fiction. [1. Depressions—1929—Fiction. 2. Education—Fiction. 3. Family life—Fiction. 4. Perseverance (Ethics)—Fiction. 5.Gratitude—Fiction.] I. Ellison, Chris, ill. II. Title.
PZ7.Y8664Luc 2008
[Fic]—dc22 2007035123

Author's Note

The Great Depression was an economic disaster that began in 1929 and lasted over a decade. Thousands of businesses shut down, leaving millions of people without jobs. Banks closed and people lost their savings. Many families lost their homes, unable to pay rent or mortgages. Items previously taken for granted became unaffordable luxuries as people struggled just to buy food and clothes.

Approximately 20,000 rural schools also closed during the Depression. Many more reduced the length of the school year to cut costs. In addition, numerous children dropped out of school to help their families earn money.

In 1933 President Franklin Delano Roosevelt established the Civilian Conservation Corps (CCC). The CCC provided jobs for over 3.4 million men at over 4,000 work camps. Most CCC workers were 18-25 years old, but older men, like Ruth's father, were hired to train younger ones. Each worker earned $30 a month but was required to send $25 home to their families. The CCC planted over three billion trees, built 41,000 bridges and 125,000 miles of roads, strung 89,000 miles of telephone wire, and restored over 4,000 historic buildings. These hardworking men also improved our national and state parks by building picnic areas, cabins, swimming pools, and 13,000 miles of hiking trails. Much of what the CCC built still exists today.

When writing *The Lucky Star*, I specifically chose the books won in the spelling bee and the main character's name so they would also be consistent with the time period. *The Book of Knowledge* was a popular 20-volume set of children's books sold at that time. "Ruth" was one of the top ten girl names of the 1920s, when my character would have been born. I chose it in honor of my Aunt Ruth, who was a child during the Great Depression.

"We don't have much," Momma said, "but remember, there's always someone who is worse off than you are. So count your lucky stars that you've got what you've got."

Momma was always counting her lucky stars. Poppa was one of them, and Ruth and her little sister, Janie, too. Their little house was a star, and so were their clothes, the food on the table, and even the fact that they had a table.

Momma's sky was filled with stars. On summer nights sitting on the porch steps, she would point up to the sky and say, "See that lucky star twinkling there? That one's for the breeze that kept the house cool today. And that one over there," she said, pointing in a different direction, "I'm counting that one for the shoes the neighbor gave you."

Ruth looked down at her feet and the old brown leather shoes. They were scuffed and creased, and the bottoms were nearly worn through. Baling twine laced through the eyes instead of shoelaces.

When the neighbor handed them to Ruth to try on, Momma said, "Count your lucky stars they are too big for you. You won't grow out of them for a long time."

SPELL G BEE

Ruth didn't see Momma's stars. Her sky was big and dark, pitch black. For Ruth, there were no lucky stars shining down on them. Ruth was ten years old and was supposed to be going into the fifth grade. But it was 1933 and the Great Depression had swept the nation. Millions of people were out of work. Millions of families had very little money for food and clothes, and there was nothing left for luxuries.

September was just a week away when Ruth found out that school was a luxury. The town could not afford to pay teachers or keep the school building lit and warm. Ruth would not be going to fifth grade.

"Count your lucky stars," said Momma, "that you were the star pupil in last spring's spelling bee."

Ruth looked at the collection of big red books with *The Book of Knowledge* written on the spines in shiny gold letters. They sat in their place on the shelf above her bed. Poppa had built that shelf especially for the books. They were her prize for spelling the word "perseverance."

Ruth knew all about perseverance. It meant to keep trying, even if things were hard. These times required a lot of perseverance.

Momma looked at the books, too. "You can use them to keep up with your studies," she continued, "until they can open the school again."

Ruth knew Momma was trying to cheer her up. Ruth loved school and Momma and Poppa were both proud of her.

"You are going to be our shining star," Ruth remembered Poppa saying. "You'll be the first in our family to graduate from high school.

"And Janie," he said, tickling Ruth's little sister, "it won't be long before you shine in school, too."

Ruth took one of the big red books off the shelf, trying to hold back tears. By doing well in school, she dreamed she would become the brightest star that glittered in Momma's sky. But now that light had been shut off.

How am I going to continue with my studies without a teacher? thought Ruth.

Janie reached out for the book and Ruth handed it to her. She watched as Janie curled up with it on the bed the two sisters shared.

Janie was supposed to start school this year. How would Janie learn to read?

Ruth looked at Momma and knew she was trying to think of another lucky star.

Ruth loved her mother, but she knew Momma would not be able to teach her. Momma had not gone to school and did not know how to read or write. Poppa could have been her teacher. He had been all the way through the sixth grade, but now he was not there to help.

That had been another star that had turned black.

Like millions of others, Poppa had lost his job.

He had worked at the lumberyard for years, but with the bad times people stopped building. Then the lumberyard owners could not afford to keep him. Both he and Momma found odd jobs to keep food on the table and a roof over their heads, but it had become harder and harder to do.

One day late last April, Poppa came home excited. He had a job! The Civilian Conservation Corps that President Roosevelt had developed to give young men jobs had hired Poppa because of his experience in the lumber industry. He would train and supervise young workers coming into the Corps.

The whole family was excited. Now they would not have to worry about becoming homeless like so many others.

But the good news brought sadness as well.

Although Poppa had a job, he would not be able to stay at home. He would be sent off to a work camp hundreds of miles away. Poppa said he didn't like the idea of being away from his family, but he would be paid thirty dollars a month and would send twenty-five of it home.

"Count your lucky stars," Momma said upon hearing the news. "With the money you make, there will still be a home for you to come back to."

But when Poppa went away, it felt like another star burned out of Ruth's sky.

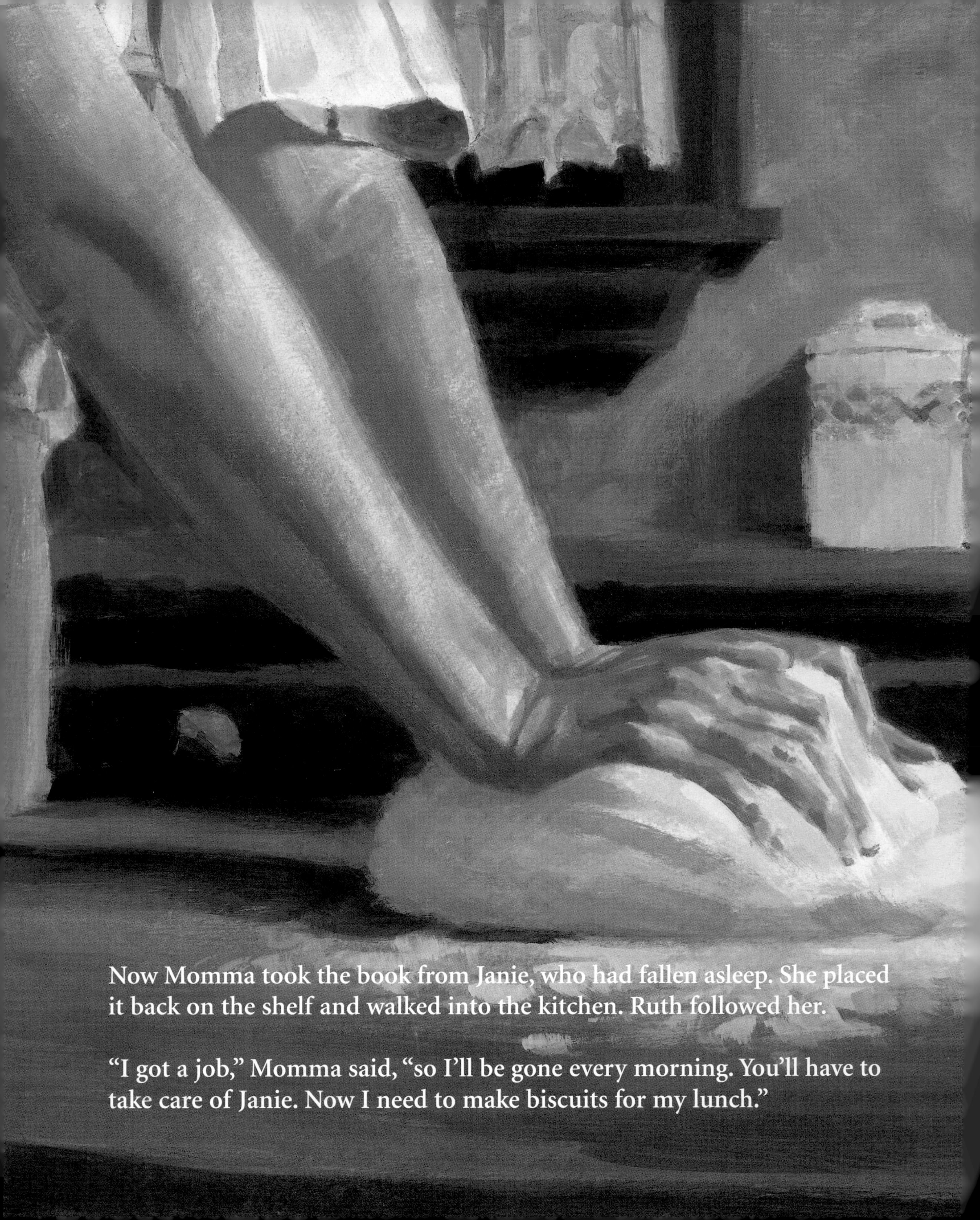

Now Momma took the book from Janie, who had fallen asleep. She placed it back on the shelf and walked into the kitchen. Ruth followed her.

“I got a job,” Momma said, “so I’ll be gone every morning. You’ll have to take care of Janie. Now I need to make biscuits for my lunch.”

Ruth sat down at the table and watched as Momma mixed flour, shortening, water, and baking powder together. She sprinkled a little flour onto the table. As Momma kneaded the dough, Ruth ran her finger through the flour on the table. She was glad Momma found a job but it didn't cheer her up about the school closing.

While the biscuits were baking, Momma and Ruth walked out onto the porch and sat down on the steps.

The sun was going down and soon the sky would be filled with dots of light. They sat there quietly watching the orange and red sky. As the colors faded, the first tiny star began to twinkle ever so slightly. Momma pointed to it.

“See that star. That star is dim now, but watch it. It will grow brighter. That star is you, Ruth. You will be the lucky star for Janie. And don’t worry. I know there’s a lucky star out there for you, too. It will come with time.”

With that, Momma kissed Ruth on the forehead and went into the house.

Ruth sat and looked at the star. As the sky darkened, it became brighter and brighter. Ruth thought about what Momma said and wondered what she meant. Once the sky had completely darkened, Ruth went in the house, too.

She lay down in bed next to Janie, watching the star through the window. Just as she was about to fall asleep, Momma's words whispered in her head. "You will be the lucky star for Janie."

Ruth looked at Janie sleeping peacefully beside her and smiled as an idea became as bright as a star in her mind.

Momma left early the next morning. Ruth helped Janie get dressed and then she started fixing biscuits for breakfast.

Just as Momma had done the night before, Ruth mixed flour, shortening, water, and baking powder together. She sprinkled a little flour onto the table and kneaded the dough. Then Ruth patted the dough flat with the palm of her hand. Janie used the lip of a jelly jar glass to cut out the round biscuits.

Ruth put the biscuits on a pan and into the oven to bake. Instead of cleaning the table, though, she lightly spread the leftover flour across the table, forming a thin layer of dust.

Janie watched Ruth curiously.

When the biscuits were done, the two girls ate them out on the front porch.

"You won't be able to start school this year," Ruth told Janie between bites, "because they closed it, but count your lucky stars you have me! I will be your teacher. Now, run along and bring back your friends. They need a lucky star, too. Tell their mommas they need to be here every day right after breakfast."

Soon Janie and her friends were gathered in the kitchen around the flour-covered table.

"I know nobody can afford pencils and paper, but count your lucky stars we have a little flour," announced Ruth.

Placing her hand over Janie's hand, Ruth guided Janie's finger through the flour.

"Go down and curve like an upside-down cane. That's the letter *J*," Ruth patiently told her.

"Now make an *A* like this," she said, guiding Janie's finger.

"Next, a zigzag for an *N*. The *I* is easy. Just make a straight line," Ruth said as she made Janie's finger slide through the flour.

"The *E* is last, like this," Ruth stated.

Ruth let go of Janie's hand. All the children looked at the letters formed in the flour.

"That's your name. *J-A-N-I-E*. Janie," Ruth exclaimed.

Ruth smiled at Janie and Janie smiled back.

JANIE

Then Ruth helped each child write his or her own name in the flour. Soon, names were all over the table.

“Now go home and practice whenever your mommas make biscuits,” Ruth told the children.

AMES

Momma's job lasted through the fall and winter and into the warm days of spring.

Each morning Ruth made biscuits and each morning the children came soon after breakfast. Ruth missed going to school but she loved teaching the children. They learned to write letters and numbers in the flour. They learned to read and write words and sentences.

Some days they sat on the porch. Using pebbles, Ruth taught them to count, add, and subtract. Then they went back in the house and learned to write arithmetic problems in the flour.

The best part of each day Ruth saved for the very last.

After their lessons, Ruth reached up to the shelf above her bed and pulled down one of the big red books. With the children gathered around her, she opened the book and read aloud. She read about history and people and places. She read about plants and animals, oceans and mountains. And she read about stars.

Each day, when she finished reading, Ruth turned to the page that showed a picture of a vast black sky dotted with twinkling stars, and each day she whispered quietly, "Count your lucky stars."

Spring was gone and now it was summertime. Almost a whole year had passed.

Ruth still wore the old brown shoes, although they fit a little better now. Poppa was still away from home, but the money came every month. The school would still be closed in the fall but Janie and the other children were learning to read and write.

And now, at night when Ruth sat out on the porch steps with Momma, she saw how the sky was filled with stars.